STUDY GUIDE FOR
RESUSCITATED

A COVID-19 TRAGEDY

MERRY CHRISTIAN

WestBow Press books may be ordered through booksellers or by contacting:

WestBow Press
A Division of Thomas Nelson & Zondervan
1663 Liberty Drive
Bloomington, IN 47403
www.westbowpress.com
1 (866) 928-1240

ISBN: 978-1-9736-9384-0 (sc)
ISBN: 978-1-9736-9385-7 (e)

Print information available on the last page.

WestBow Press rev. date: 06/13/2020

WESTBOW
PRESS®
A DIVISION OF THOMAS NELSON
& ZONDERVAN

INDEX

INTRODUCTION TO GENRE

What causes you to read a book? Some readers have a preferable author, and most readers have a preferable **genre.** Genre refers to the style, the form, and the content of the writing. Readers can be drawn to content that interests, informs, and/or entertains them. There are four main genres in literature: poetry, prose, drama, and nonfiction. **Prose** refers to communication that is written using everyday speech. Newspapers, textbooks, and novels are examples of prose. Newspapers, textbooks, and **nonfiction** differ from prose, poetry, and drama in that the first is true or factual. Prose, poetry, and drama are works of **fiction** because they are not entirely true or factual, although there could be many truths or facts within the manuscript.

A **novel** is a long prose composition which is usually published in book form. Most readers narrow their novel choices to favorite **subgenres** such as folklore, mythology, mystery, romance, thriller, diary, historical fiction, science fiction, and realistic fiction.

When selecting a hard copy of a book, whether hardcover or softcover, a reader will be drawn by the book's cover. Hardcover books often have a dust jacket, a removable paper covering with flaps which gives information about the book. The author's photograph and background, the book's summary, and a book excerpt may be some of the information found on the dust cover and helps a reader decide if they want to read the book.

Electronic books are marketed using much the same information via technology. Each author submits to the publisher key search words which match the content of their book. These keywords are used by libraries and distributors to direct a reader to the book's page. Here the reader will find much the same information about the book that is found on a dust cover.

After you finish reading *Resuscitated – A COVID-19 Tragedy,* use specifics from the book to explain why the novel is realistic fiction.

THE PLOT

The **plot** is the events or the action of the novel. In a typical story, the plot follows a pattern of introduction, rising action, climax, falling action, and denouement. The **introduction** gives the background information that the reader needs to be able to understand what is about to take place in the story. The **rising action** is the events that create interest and suspense. It is during this part of the novel that a **conflict** is introduced. The point at which this conflict becomes the most exciting or strongest is called the **climax.** The narrative after the climax is the **falling action.** During this part of the story the author will tie up all the loose ends. The part of the story that deals with the resolution or the final outcome of the conflict is the **denouement.**

What event do you think is the climax of this novel?

THE SETTING

The setting of a novel includes **when** and **where** the action occurred. Sometimes the setting is precise; sometimes the setting is vague. Often the reader must gather hints as she reads to determine the "when" and the "where" of a story.

When did *Resuscitated – A COVID-19 Tragedy* did place?

Where did *Resuscitated – A COVID-19 Tragedy* take place?

POINT OF VIEW

The **point of view** of a novel is the method an author uses to relate the story. One can determine the point of view by asking the question, "Who is telling the story?" If the main character expresses himself or herself using first person pronouns such as I, me, my, and mine, then the point of view is **first person point of view.** If the narrator uses second person pronouns such as you or your, then the story is **second person point of view.** Narratives using third person pronouns such as he and she are in the **third person point of view.** There are two types of third person point of view. One is called third person **limited** point of view when the story is told by a narrator who does not have insights into a character's thoughts. The third person **omniscient** point of view is told by a narrator who knows everything about the characters including their thoughts. Omniscient means "all knowing" like God who knows everything.

In what point of view is *Resuscitated – A COVID-19 Tragedy* written?

CONFLICT

The struggle or challenge in the story that a character faces is called the **conflict.** There may be more than one conflict in a narrative, and different characters may be challenged by different adversaries. Most conflicts or struggles can be categorized as man vs man, man vs nature, or as man vs himself. The first two types of conflict are self-explanatory. The conflict of man vs himself is an inner struggle, a psychological conflict, that the character is trying to answer. Most conflicts are resolved during the denouement of the novel, although some authors leave a conflict unresolved for a **hanging ending** to their book.

Write several paragraphs about the conflict(s) in *Resuscitated – A COVID-19 Tragedy.* For the conflicts(s) name the two opposing forces and use examples to argue whether the author resolved the struggle(s).

HOOKS

A **hook** in literature is a deliberate effort by the writer to initially engage the reader and stimulate them to continue reading. Hooks are found at the beginning of prose and sometimes throughout the composition to continue to motivate the reader to finish the novel. List the three hooks found in chapter 1 of *Resuscitated – A COVID-19 Tragedy.*

You will find unfinished sentences, questions, or thoughts in *Resuscitated – A COVID-19 Tragedy* that the author has used to keep you hooked in the narrative. As you continue reading *Resuscitated – A COVID-19 Tragedy,* write down any other hooks that you find in the story.

FLASHBACK AND FORESHADOW

Both flashbacks and foreshadows are narrative that is out of chronological order in a story. A **flashback** gives the reader information that occurred before the novel began. Flashbacks in the form of dreams or reminisces are often woven into a plot to help the reader understand the characters or the action of the novel. While a flashback happened in the past, a **foreshadow** hints about something that is going to happen in the future in the plot. Foreshadows build suspense and are often very subtle and may be missed by a reader until the event that had been foreshadowed actually happens.

What flashbacks can you find in *Resuscitated – A COVID-19 Tragedy?*

What foreshadows can you find in *Resuscitated – A COVID-19 Tragedy?*

THEME

All authors write for a purpose; they have an idea to express, a message, or a moral. Like a good joke teller who never explains why his joke is funny, a writer lets his composition speak for itself as to the theme. Short writings often have just one theme, but longer manuscripts may have several themes. When more than one theme is expressed, one is usually the dominant theme or main purpose of the writing.

Write several paragraphs about the theme(s) of *Resuscitated – A COVID-19 Tragedy*. Use specific examples from the story to support your choice of the theme(s). If you argue that the novel has more than one theme, then give textual proofs as to which theme is the dominant theme, that is the most important idea that the author is trying to convey.

FIGURATIVE LANGUAGE

When writers use a word or phrase which cannot be taken literally, that is according to the definition(s) of the word(s), then they are using figurative language. The meaning of the word or words used has additional meaning beyond the definitions or may not appear to have any meaning related to the definitions of each word. Readers must be fully engaged to comprehend these figures of speech, as they give nuances and depth to the meaning that the author is trying to convey. There are over one hundred figures of speech. The most common are simile, metaphor, personification, hyperbole, understatement, irony, oxymoron, allusion, and idiom.

SIMILE

Simile is a figure of speech that makes a comparison between two things that are not alike but do share some similarities. These different words or ideas are connected by the word "like" or "as." In the example "teeth as white as milk," the reader knows that both teeth and milk are white, but using this simile emphasizes how really white the teeth are. Another example: Her eyes were like sparkling sapphires.

Find a simile in both chapter one and chapter 6.

METAPHOR

Metaphor is a simile which compares two things that are not alike but do share some similarities. A metaphor differs from a simile in that the words "like" or "as" are **not** used. "I am the good shepherd" is a metaphor.

Find the metaphor in the opening sentence of *Resuscitated – A COVID-19 Tragedy*.

PERSONIFICATION

Personification is a figure of speech that uses human qualities to describe nonhuman things.

We have long personified the natural world as Mother Nature and the United States government as Uncle Sam. **Anthropomorphism** is very similar to personification. In this case, the writer makes an animal or object behave and appear like it is a human being as in the children's classic *The Little Engine that Could*.

Find as least three examples of personification in chapters 1-3 in *Resuscitated– A COVID-19 Tragedy*.

HYPERBOLE AND UNDERSTATEMENT

Hyperbole is an exaggeration that obviously is not true. Authors use hyperbole to emphasize a thought. Examples: Your purse weighs a ton. The horse broke from the gate faster than a lightning bolt.

Understatement is the antonym of hyperbole. Example: She had lost so much weight that she was light as a feather.

Find the hyperbole in chapter 3 in *Resuscitated– A COVID-19 Tragedy*.

Find the hyperbole in chapter 11.

IRONY

Irony is using words or developing situations which mean the opposite of what a reader would expect. <u>Situational irony</u> is when the opposite result occurs from what is to be expected. (example: The police station was robbed of its petty cash.) <u>Verbal irony</u> is saying one thing and meaning the opposite. (example: The assembly instructions were as clear as mud.)

Find the two ironies in chapter 1 of *Resuscitated – A COVID-19 Tragedy*.

Write an explanatory paragraph about the irony in the book's ending.

OXYMORON

Oxymoron is a figure of speech in which two words of opposite meanings are used together.

Examples: foolish wisdom; clearly confused

Find two oxymorons in *Resuscitated– A COVID-19 Tragedy,* one in each of chapters 16 and 27.

An **idiom** is a phrase that means something different than the definition of the individual words.

The English language is full of idioms, and it is this figure of speech that often gives foreign language persons difficulty when learning English. Idioms are more interesting methods of conveying ideas. Consider these idioms and their meanings.

I can't seem to wrap my head around that...................means I don't understand that

That was a blessing in disguise....................something good that seemed bad at first

Let's call it a day...Let's stop working.

Explain the following idioms (underlined) found in *Resuscitated– A COVID-19 Tragedy*.

1. Chapter 12 "<u>I'll cross that bridge when I come to it</u>. Good-bye," Sarah snapped back and shakily hung up.

2. Chapter 15 "I try to call when nothing else will interrupt our time together. <u>I'm all ears</u>."

3. Chapter 16 "I think that <u>the cat is out of the bag</u> now."

4. Chapter 28 " I hope that Uncle Sam doesn't defend mandatory tracking by <u>the ends justifying the means</u>."

5. Chapter 27 "Sarah was determined <u>to soldier on</u>."

ALLUSION

An **allusion** is an indirect, brief reference to something that is widely-known about history, culture, or literature. The author assumes that the reader has prior knowledge that would help her understand at what the author was hinting. An allusion adds unwritten information to the text. For instance, in the allusion - Bart was a Solomon in all of his classes.- the reader would expect Bart to be as wise as Solomon (Note: If a character were named Solomon in a novel and that character was very foolish, then it would be situational irony.)

The following names of characters in *Resuscitated – A COVID-19 Tragedy* are Biblical allusions. Explain the hidden meaning behind each character's name and how that character was like their Biblical namesake.

Stephen

Joseph

Tabitha

Herod

Explain these other allusions (underlined) in *Resuscitated – A COVID-19 Tragedy.*

1. "It is so reassuring that there are <u>Golden Rule</u> people in the world today."

2. "The new normal at grocery stores and other retail outlets mirrored the <u>Draconian</u> measures taken by the Transportation and Security Administration at airports after 9-11."

3. "The chances of an <u>Orwellian</u> society are becoming more and more tangible."

4. "These <u>Rosie-the-Riveter</u> classmates worked in isolation but in cooperation."

5. "Invisible COVID-19 attacked the <u>Titanic</u> sports world."

ALLITERATION, ASSONANCE, ONOMATOPOEIA

Alliteration, assonance, and onomatopoeia are writing techniques that use phonetics to embellish and increase the pleasing sound of the script. **<u>Alliteration</u>** is the deliberate and noticeable writing technique that repeats identical, initial consonant sounds in adjacent words or two or more words within a phrase. The closer the alliteration is in the text the more effective it is. Tongue twisters are good examples of alliteration as is the term "tongue twister." You are probably familiar with these classic tongue twisters: "Sally sells seashells by the seashore" and "Peter Piper picked a peck of pickled peppers." Not only are alliterations pleasing to the ear, they also can be a mnemonic device. There are alliterative sports teams' names (Philadelphia Phillies), consumer product names (Coca-Coca Classic), and movie and book titles (*Pride and Prejudice).*

There are dozens of alliterations in *Resuscitated – A COVID-19 Tragedy.* Some of these are adjacent words, and some are separated by other words. Examples include: "women stood staring at each other" (chapter 3); "Sarah looked at her watch and waited" (chapter 3); "the bushytails would be bounding beneath the budding trees looking for overlooked, buried acorns from last winter's cache" (chapter 14).

Chapter one of *Resuscitated-A COVID-19 Tragedy* has over two dozen alliterations. List a dozen of them below. Find and circle the alliteration that begins with two different consonants but qualifies as an alliteration because both consonant beginnings have the same sound.

Assonance is closely related to alliteration and is the repetition of identical or similar vowel sounds in adjacent words or within phrases. Not only are the two tongue twisters examples of alliterations, but they also illustrate assonance. "Peter Piper picked a peck of pickled peppers" repeats the short i and the short e sounds; "Sally sells seashells beside the seashore" repeats the short e sound and the long e sound. Assonance differs from rhyme in that rhyme is a repetition of both vowel and consonant sounds. Chapter one of *Resuscitated – A COVID-19 Tragedy* closes with, "Suddenly she felt weak, slid to the carpet, wept, and slept." The ending of this sentence is a rhyme and not an example of assonance.

Find the example of assonance in chapter 1 of *Resuscitated - – A COVID-19 Tragedy.*

Onomatopoeia is using a word that sounds like the noise that it is representing.

Splish-splash and buzz are examples of onomatopoeia. Find an example of onomatopoeia in chapter I of *Resuscitated – A COVID-19 Tragedy.*

WORKSHEET ON ALLITERATION, ASSONANCE, AND ONOMATOPOEIA

On the line in front of the following excerpts from *Resuscitated – A COVID-19 Tragedy*, identify whether the phrase illustrates alliteration (**AL**), assonance (**AS**), or onomatopoeia (**ON**). Some phrases may be examples of two literary sound techniques.

1. _____ Somewhere a strutting turkey gurgled his gobble.

2. _____ pastures with cattle placidly grazing their fenced bounds

3. _____ The melodious music lifted her spirit.

4. _____ Edna always beamed and bubbled in their presence.

5. _____ the debilitating, depressing, and devastating ravages of dementia

6. _____ the pipping of spring peepers in the wetlands

7. _____ interrupted her musings as Jeannie maneuvered a wheelchair into the room

8. _____ drive the rural roads for a country block

9. _____ to profusely thank everyone for the plethora of pantry foods

10. _____ Blackbirds were already trilling in her bottomland.

11. _____ even the soft pitter-patter of raindrops against the windows

12. _____ Flora and fauna together performed an unforgettable, indelible crescendo.

13. _____ Daryl would tussle and scuffle with the puppy.

14. _____ Rewind to fast forward.

15. _____ Sarah tried to occupy her mind and time.

16. _____ Oreo yelped a loud meow.

17. _____ after being scanned, searched, and stamped with invisible ink

18. _____ an approved visitor's list before admittance during visiting hours

19. _____ She heard the jangling rumble of the steel gurney.

20. _____ Still a shudder traversed her spine as Stephen's incarceration suddenly became palpable.

LITERARY LICENSE

Literary license is the deliberate act of a writer not following standard grammar, punctuation, and spelling rules. In *Resuscitated – A COVID-19 Tragedy,* Merry Christian made up words, used words incorrectly, and misspelled words. Below are examples of literary license taken by the author. Read the word in context and explain why you think that the author did not follow formal conventions in her writing.

1. ("Bushytails" is not a real word.)
   "It was a warm, cozy day, and Sarah knew that the bushytails would be bounding beneath the budding trees looking for overlooked, buried acorns from last winter's cache."

2. ("Purrball" is not a real word.)
   In a conscious effort to prolong that comforting dream, and carrying the furry purrball, Sarah arose and methodically visited every nook and cranny of her abode.

3. (The definition of abandonee is: one that holds or claims abandoned property.)
   The vow that she had made to visit abandonees at the nursing center was sacrosanct.

4. Underline the word or words from these excerpts from the novel that the author has written using literary license. Why do you think that the author used these created words?
   "I couldn't control my laughter! I assured Daryl that the growling was puppy-speak for 'Wow! This is great fun!'" Sarah chuckled.
   "When Maria asked the employee why Shep kept shaking his head, the girl said it was dog-speak, 'Play with me.'"

PSEUDONYM

The term **pseudonym** means "false name" and is also known as a pen name. You are probably familiar with several famous authors who have used pseudonyms. Samuel Clemens wrote under the pen name Mark Twain, and Mary Ann Evans wrote under the pen name George Eliot. The latter adopted a male pseudonym to give her writings a better chance of success, as women writers were not taken seriously in the 1800s. Today a whistleblower may use a pseudonym for obvious reasons.

Do you think that Merry Christian, the author of *Resuscitated – A COVID-19 Tragedy,* is a pen name? Why or why not?

Can you think of any reason for the author to use a pen name to write this book?

VOCABULARY EXERCISES FOR CHAPTERS 1-10

Below are phrases or sentences from the novel *Resuscitated – A COVID-19 Tragedy.* Within that sentence is a parenthetical word and blank. Study the parenthetical word in context. Select a synonym for the word from the word bank, and write it on the blank line.

goodbye	empathetic	elatedly	understanding	weakly
scolding	passionately	perishable	contemplated	pondered
helpful	fervently	questions	sentimental	comforting
tumor	virtuously	substitute	promised	resided

1. For this (mortal _____) life, they faced each sunrise without hope.

2. Sarah parked her car and (meditated _____) a moment.

3. ... the (obliging _____) gentleman carried her piece of luggage to the door and bid her adieu.

4. ... the obliging gentleman carried her piece of luggage to the door and bid her (adieu_____).

5. Instantly the purring machine would start, and warm, forgiving emotions would overtake Sarah's (chastisement _____) thoughts.

6. Slowly getting to her feet, Sarah made her way to the stairs and, clutching the handrail, (feebly _____) navigated to the first floor.

7. They held (nostalgic _____) memories for Sarah, but the children may have felt no warm attachment to them.

8. To help us with your perspective, we talked with our parents, for they would be more (empathetic _____) about you leaving your home.

9. Since your new neighbors have been so (compassionate _____) and understanding of my situation, I think that they will fill our shoes easily.

10. Sarah made a cup of tea and again (mused _____) about the blessed freedom of enjoying a cup of tea anytime she wished.

11. ...these she would always carry with her wherever she (sojourned _____).

12. I prayed (fervently_____) about it and decided to offer you the treatment.

13. I (vowed _____) that I would work the rest of my life trying to cure cancer and heal other mothers in memory of my mother.

14. You are frustrated because you so righteously (_____) and earnestly care for your patients and saving the lives of even strangers.

15. In retrospect I suppose that I was using each of you as a (surrogate _____) for helping my mom," admitted Stephen.

16. I have been questioned by authorities but have been able to answer queries (_____) rather ambiguously.

17. I will pray unceasingly and (passionately_____) for you and this complicated state of affairs.

18. Sarah (ecstatically _____) grabbed Oreo from Hazel and hugged the furball tight.

19. Think of all the research, drugs, equipment, laboratory tests, doctors' consultations, surgeons' fees, hospital stays, and (palliative _____) care that my simple pill would abolish.

20. Now after years of successful, thorough (oncology _____) research, I have determined that cancers are caused by an obscure, mutating virus.

VOCABULARY EXERCISES FOR CHAPTERS 11-20

Below are phrases or sentences from the novel *Resuscitated – A COVID-19 Tragedy*. Within that sentence is a parenthetical word and blank. Study the parenthetical word in context. Select a synonym for the word from the word bank, and write it on the blank line.

protector	stroll	stipulation	required	downcast
confused	dejectedly	enthusiastic	puzzling	recovery
rebirth	summons	upsetting	weakness	ordered
sadness	noticeable	overabundance	filled	edge

1. The medicine of love was escalating her (recuperation _____).

2. She sat motionless with anger, confusion, and indecision. She must contact Stephen about this (traumatizing _____) exchange.

3. Ma'am, do you know that the FDA can get a (subpoena _____) and compel you to submit to this directive?

4. Sarah took the opportunity to profusely thank everyone for the (plethora _____) of pantry foods that she had found on her doorstep.

5. This plethora of spring (renaissance _____) steadied her and levitated her spirits.

6. Sarah positioned herself on the (periphery _____) of the audience that was watching the Girl Scout performance.

7. Yes, I remember when Daryl became (despondent _____), and I knew that something was bothering him.

8. To lift him out of his (melancholy _____), I suggested that he go play tug-of- war with the puppy.

9. Looking back over his shoulder and then toward the end of the driveway, it was obvious that the pet was (conflicted _____).

10. Shep's (exuberant _____), welcome-home greeting for Maria was the nail in the coffin.

11. The last small gift was set before Sarah with an (enigmatic _____) caveat from Bonnie attached.

12. The last small gift was set before Sarah with an enigmatic (caveat _____) from Bonnie attached.

13. Sarah then and there vowed to be an (advocate _____) henceforth for those imprisoned there.

14. Was today's (frailty _____) a passing infirmity or was Edna's health on a precipitous, downward spiral?

15. The drizzle had staunched, and the sweet-smelling freshness of new growth (permeated_____) the air.

16. Without a word, Sarah (disconsolately _____) walked the gloomy, cloudy tunnel back to the lobby and out to her car.

17. Joseph had to take one last (amble _____) around their property.

18. Would she have wanted (compulsory _____) visits from her children as a Chinese law mandated in China?

19. Would she have wanted compulsory visits from her children as a Chinese law (mandated _____) in China?

20. Mid-stride the dog halted and, then with one giant, whining leap, collided with Sarah who by now was kneeling on the pavement with arms outstretched. It was a (palpable _____) reunion of love.

Below are phrases or sentences from the novel *Resuscitated – A COVID-19 Tragedy*. Within that sentence is a parenthetical word and blank. Study the parenthetical word in context. Select a synonym for the word from the word bank, and write it on the blank line.

evaluated	inform	goodness	begging	recuperating
acquitted	refuge	arraignment	isolate	alleviation
microbe	line	revived	indirect	imprisonment
dying	writ	palpable	forcefully	absolve

1. I am certainly going to do everything in my power to have him exonerated," Sarah said (vehemently _____).

2. I am certainly going to do everything in my power to have him (exonerated _____).

3. She asked God for the strength and the wisdom to do everything in her power to comfort, support, and (vindicate _____) Dr. Bush.

4. Jared and Jessica have received a (summons _____), and it is my understanding that the FDA tried to serve you with a writ on Friday.

5. The righteous indignation which all three felt about their savior's (indictment _____) and incarceration was palpable.

6. The righteous indignation which all three felt about their savior's indictment and (incarceration _____) was palpable.

7. Sarah (appraised _____) Stephen's handwriting which he had penned on the inmate's portion of the Visitor Information Form.

8. At the announcement for the next visiting group to move to the screening area, Dr. Bush's (resuscitated _____) patients complied.

9. Inside a (queue _____) formed as signs directed that inmates and visitors would be assigned seating.

10. Stephen was just a number here, but there were some (subtle _____) differences in treatment.

11. Only minutes later at his appearing did the perception become (tangible _____) when Stephen entered the room in prisoner's garb.

12. The stark contrast from the purity and (benevolence _____) of a doctor's white uniform to the shaming, humbling prisoner's uniform shafted Sarah's conscience.

13. While seniors babysat, mothers completed household chores for those (convalescing _____) at home.

14. The lawyer did (apprise _____) them of the results of the hair analysis completed by the lab.

15. Being at great danger to (succumbing _____) to COVID-19, Sue's mother could not risk allowing her daughter to quarantine at home.

16. Being at great danger to succumbing to COVID-19, Sue's mother could not risk allowing her daughter to (quarantine _____) at home.

17. Sarah considered offering Sue (sanctuary _____) for her self-isolation, but sixty-eight-year-old Sarah was in a vulnerable group herself.

18. I have been catching up on all of the coronavirus information and reading medical reports about this (pathogen _____).

19. Scientists were using the diagram to reject or endorse (mitigation _____) policies proposed by government leaders.

20. The leaders at the epicenter of this pandemic have been (beseeching _____) volunteer medical professionals to come and help them in this crisis.

GLOSSARY

adieu	goodbye
admonish	rebuke, scold, reprimand
advocate	protector
amble	stroll, ramble
appraise	evaluate
apprise	inform, notify
azure	bright blue
benevolence	kindness, goodness, goodwill
beseech	implore, beg
caveat	stipulation, limitation
chastisement	scolding
compassionate	sympathetic, empathetic, understanding
compulsory	mandatory, required
conflicted	confused
convalesce	recuperate, recover
despondent	discouraged, disheartened, downhearted
disconsolate	unhappy, downcast, dejected
ecstatic	elated, enraptured
empathy	sympathy, understanding, compassion
enigmatic	puzzling
exonerate	absolve, acquit
exuberant	luxuriant, lush; ebullient, enthusiastic, excited
feebly	weakly, frailly, shakily
fervently	passionately, enthusiastically
frailty	weakness, infirmity
hospice	a home providing care for the sick or terminally ill
incarceration	imprisonment, confinement, detention
indelible	ineradicable, unremovable
indictment	accusation, arraignment
infirmity	frailty, weakness
interment	burial, committal, entombment
malevolent	malicious, spiteful, wicked
mandated	ordered, required by law
meditate	contemplate, ponder

melancholy	sadness, downhearted, sorrowful
mitigate	alleviate, lessen, reduce
mortal	perishable
mortality	death, dying
muse	ponder, consider
nostalgic	sentimental
obituary	death notice
obliging	helpful, accommodating, considerate
oncology	study and treatment of tumors
palliative	soothing, comforting, alleviating
palpable	perceptible, noticeable, tangible
passionate	fervent, zealous, intense
pathogen	bacterium, virus, or microorganism that can cause disease
periphery	edge, boundary, border
permeated	saturated, filled
pestilence	plague, epidemic, pandemic
plethora	overabundance
providence	the protective care of God or of nature as a spiritual power
quarantine	isolation, confinement
queried	inquired, questioned
queue	line, file
recuperation	convalescence, recovery
remedial	counteractive, corrective, curative
renaissance	rebirth
resuscitated	revive, resurrect, restore
righteously	rightly, virtuously
sanctuary	refuge, haven, shelter
sojourn	visit, stopover, residence
staccato	series of short, sharply separated sounds
subpoena	summons; a writ ordering a person to attend a court
subtle	indirect
succumb	to die
summons	subpoena, writ, warrant, arraignment
surrogate	substitute
tangible	palpable, real
traumatic	shocking, disturbing, upsetting
vehemence	forcefulness, violence
vindicate	acquit, absolve, clear
vowed	promised, swore

Printed in the United States
By Bookmasters